Annabelle's Un-Birthday

Annabelle's Un-Birthday

by Steven Kroll
illustrated by Gail Owens

Macmillan Publishing Company
New York
Collier Macmillan Canada
Toronto
Maxwell Macmillan International Publishing Group
New York   Oxford   Singapore   Sydney

To my wife, Abigail,
for helping to strike the spark,
and to my editor, Judith Whipple,
for her encouragement.

Text copyright © 1991 by Steven Kroll
Illustrations copyright © 1991 by Gail Owens
Macmillan Publishing Company
866 Third Avenue
New York, NY 10022

Collier Macmillan Canada, Inc.
1200 Eglinton Avenue East
Suite 200
Don Mills, Ontario M3C 3N1

First edition
Printed in the United States of America

10   9   8   7   6   5   4   3   2   1

The text of this book is set in 13 pt. Meridien.
The illustrations are rendered in pencil
Book design by Christy Hale

Library of Congress Cataloging-in-Publication Data
    Annabelle's un-birthday / by Steven Kroll : illustrated by Gail Owens. — 1st ed.
        p.   cm.
    Summary: On the first day of school Annabelle tells her new second-grade classmates that it is her birthday and takes them to her grandmother's for an unexpected party, but she knows she must face the consequences of her fib.
    ISBN 0-02-751171-5
    [1. Honesty—Fiction. 2. Parties—Fiction. 3. Schools—Fiction. 4. Grandmothers—Fiction.] I. Owens, Gail, ill.   II. Title.   III. Title: Annabelle's unbirthday.
PZ7.K9225An F1991   [Fic]—dc20   90-24316

Contents

1 New Apartment, New School

Annabelle and her parents had just moved into a new apartment. It had two big bedrooms, a living room big enough for the sofa, Dad's rocker, and a coffee table, and a kitchen you could eat meals in. It was also on the second floor of a small brownstone on a pretty, tree-lined street. There was a carpeted stairway in the hall with a polished banister you could slide down if you were careful.

Annabelle had never seen a room like hers before. It was big enough to run around in. It was bright and cheerful, with a view of trees and gardens. Her old room had been small and dark. There had been no view at all, just an airshaft with weird smells.

And this time her mother had let her choose her own bedspread, with curtains to match! She had chosen red with white polka dots. It went wonderfully with the red and white teddy bear rug.

She had put all her dolls and bears out on shelves around the room. There was even a special bookcase for her books. Her mother had helped hang her clothes in one closet and arrange her toys in the other. She had helped her find a special spot for her toothbrush in the bathroom. There wasn't anything about the new apartment Annabelle didn't like. There were just a couple of problems with this move.

First, she'd had to leave her friends behind. No one in the new building seemed to have children. She hadn't even noticed any on the block. She knew she could visit her old friends, but what if she couldn't make new ones, not even at school?

School. That was the second problem. Because Annabelle had moved into a new school district, she had to go to a different school. The school was only two blocks away and looked perfectly all right from outside. That wasn't the problem. The problem was that everything was new and strange. The teachers didn't know her, and she didn't know them. What if they didn't like her? What if she didn't like them? What if the girls she didn't know did mean things to her or said mean things behind her back? What if there were boys who teased her or pulled her hair? Boys could be like that sometimes if they didn't like you.

There was a third problem. The first day of school was tomorrow!

Annabelle sat on her bed. She dangled her legs over the side and tossed her short blonde curls. She'd just come home from shopping with her mother. Two new sweaters and a new skirt for school. She didn't know if she would ever get to wear them. She didn't know if she could ever go to that school, she was so scared.

"Annabelle!" her mother called, "dinner's ready."

Annabelle didn't want dinner. She just wanted to be home in her old, dreary apartment getting ready to start second grade in her old, familiar school.

"Annabelle!" her mother called again.

Annabelle got off her bed and walked into the bright, cheerful, new kitchen. Instantly she felt a little better, though not much.

Her mother smiled at her. Her father was already sitting at the table. He smiled, too.

"Please sit," said her mother. "Everything will get cold."

Annabelle sat. She ate roast chicken with mixed vegetables. She ate salad and blueberry pie. But she didn't eat very much.

"What's the matter?" asked her father.

"Oh, nothing," said Annabelle.

"Something must be the matter," said her mother. "You usually eat everything in sight."

"School," said Annabelle.

"School?" said her father. "You don't even start school until tomorrow."

"I don't want to go."

Annabelle's parents looked at each other. In a moment they realized what was wrong.

"Annabelle," said her mother, "you don't have to worry about your new school. Everything will be fine. Everyone will be great."

"How do I know?"

"You can't know for sure," said her father, "but there's no

reason why you shouldn't like this school as much as the last one."

"I'm not going," said Annabelle.

"Look," said her mother, "I've got an idea. Why don't you call Grandma. She'll make you feel better."

Grandma! Grandma was the other reason why moving into the new apartment was terrific. Grandma lived only a few blocks away. Annabelle really loved her. She loved when she visited Grandma's apartment and they had tea parties and played dress-up.

Annabelle ran to the phone and dialed.

"Hello?" said her grandma's voice, as if she were a million miles away.

"Hi, Grandma, it's Annabelle."

"Hi, sweetheart, is something the matter?"

"Oh, Grandma," said Annabelle. Then she told her about school and how she felt.

Grandma listened hard. Then she explained, in her most soothing voice, how everything was bound to be all right. After that, she said the best thing of all. "Annabelle, why don't you come see me tomorrow after school? If you're having a bad time, you'll have something to look forward to. If you're having a good time, you can tell me all about it."

"Oh, good!" said Annabelle. "Oh, yes, I'll come. Oh, thank you, Grandma!"

Suddenly she felt on top of the world.

2 An Invitation

For the rest of the evening, Annabelle's thoughts were in a whirl. She was delighted she was going to see her grandma, but she was still very nervous about school. She tried to watch TV. She tried to read. She just couldn't concentrate on anything.

Before she went to bed, she laid out the clothes she would wear on the chair across the room. There was the new navy blue skirt and the light blue blouse that went so well with it. There were the neat black shoes. Everything seemed just right for the first day of school. She hoped no one would find anything to make fun of.

For a long time Annabelle lay awake in the darkness. She watched the shadows on the ceiling. She gazed at her clothes on the chair. But there were still butterflies in her stomach when she finally drifted off to sleep.

The next morning, she tried to act calm. She washed and dressed and marched into the kitchen for breakfast. It was tough to drink her juice and eat her cereal, even tougher to drink a whole glass of milk, but she took a deep breath before starting each one and somehow got through.

Her dad smiled. "You seem to be doing better this morning."

"A little."

"You're really going to like this school," said Mom.

"I hope so."

Annabelle's mother walked her to school, holding her hand all the way. Annabelle carried her notebook and pencils in her other hand. When they reached the entrance, Annabelle's mother walked her inside.

They went straight to the school office. Annabelle's mother spoke to someone called Mrs. Gordon, who was the school secretary. Mrs. Gordon told Annabelle and her mother where to find Mrs. Blake's second-grade class.

They walked down a long hallway. It had tile and bulletin boards on the walls. There were classroom doors on either side. It wasn't a very friendly hallway.

When they reached Mrs. Blake's door, it had a big paper rose taped to it. That seemed a lot more cheerful. But then Annabelle's mother was bending over and kissing her good-bye and saying, "Don't forget to have a good time today, and give my love to Grandma."

"I will," said Annabelle, feeling very small in her mother's arms.

Her mother was gone. There was the door. She was feeling so weak, she didn't know if she could open it. She turned the knob and gave a little push. Then, suddenly, the door was pulled open the rest of the way!

In front of her stood a tall, thin woman with long blonde hair and a smile that showed a lot of teeth. "Hi," she said, "I'm Mrs. Blake and welcome to second grade. Your name is . . . ?"

"Annabelle Fields," said Annabelle.

Mrs. Blake turned to the rest of the room and introduced her as the newest member of the class. "Please find yourself a seat, Annabelle," she said.

Even though it was not quite eight-thirty, the room seemed very full. Annabelle felt rooted to the spot. Finally she saw an empty seat three rows back and crept into it.

"Hi," came a whispered voice from behind her.

Annabelle turned half-around. There was a little, dark-haired girl with big brown eyes and dimples. "Hi," she whispered again, "my name's Melissa. Want to be friends?"

Suddenly everyone in class looked very nice. Mrs. Blake's smile was warm and friendly. What they were going to study this year sounded very interesting. The classroom itself felt cozy and comfortable. When you had a friend, anything was possible!

For the rest of the day, Annabelle and Melissa went everywhere together. When the class went to art and drew dinosaurs, the two girls drew them together. When they went to music and sang folk songs, Annabelle and Melissa sat side by side. At lunch, Melissa introduced Annabelle to her friends, Linda and Beth. She also talked about home.

"I've got two brothers," she said. "Both bigger than me. They don't pick on me, though. They're pretty okay."

Annabelle told about being an only child and about moving. She took big bites of her pizza as she talked. Pizza was her favorite lunch, and this pizza was especially good!

As she was finishing, a boy came up to her. She had seen him before in class. He had sandy hair falling in his eyes, and freckles.

"Hi," he said, wiping his nose on his sleeve, "I'm Ethan."

"Hi," she said. Then she looked at the girls sitting at the table, and all four of them laughed.

Ethan hurried away. Annabelle felt bad that she'd laughed, but it was nice to have a boy pay attention to her. Boys were so weird about things like that. Perhaps she could catch up with Ethan later.

And then, before she knew it, it was time to go. The boys and girls in Mrs. Blake's class were getting their things together and lining up. She and Melissa were standing side by side in the line. It was too soon for all these good things to end. She didn't want to say good-bye to Melissa yet. She didn't want to have to leave the other kids. Everyone had been so terrific. Even that boy Ethan had tried to be nice. She really liked this school. Everything had been so much fun. She was looking forward to going to her grandma's, but she didn't want to go by herself. What if all the other kids could come with her?

Annabelle stepped out of line. "Mrs. Blake?" she said.

"Yes, Annabelle."

"There's something I forgot to tell you. Today's my birthday, and the whole class is invited to a party at my grandma's!"

16

Mrs. Blake looked very surprised. "Why didn't you mention this before, Annabelle?"

Annabelle blinked. Had she just said what she thought she'd said? What was she going to do now?

She took a breath and plunged on. "I forgot to mention it because everything was so great, I—"

"Does your grandmother know she's having this party?"

"Of course. It's going to be special."

Annabelle looked back at Melissa, who was smiling and showing her dimples. "I didn't know it was your birthday," she whispered.

Annabelle shrugged.

"Well," said Mrs. Blake, "I don't want not to believe you, Annabelle, but would it be okay if I called and checked with your grandmother about this? I mean, it's not the sort of thing that happens very often."

Annabelle summoned up all her courage. "Sure, Mrs. Blake. Go ahead."

By this time, the other kids were all talking about this incredible invitation. Annabelle's birthday? A party at her grandma's? Annabelle noticed Ethan in the back whispering to his friend Tony.

"Class," Mrs. Blake said, "I want you all to stay right where you are. I'm going to call Annabelle's grandmother, and I will be right back. Annabelle will be in charge."

She left the room. Annabelle was holding her breath so hard there was a weird tingling in her ears. It was a good thing the kids seemed willing to do as they'd been told. She wouldn't have

18

known what to say if they hadn't. Then Mrs. Blake was back, shaking her head. Annabelle was terrified.

"Boys and girls," Mrs. Blake said, "you are all invited to Annabelle's birthday party at her grandma's house. It's just three blocks from school."

There was a moment of stunned silence. Then the whole class cheered.

3   On The Way

Mothers had begun arriving to pick up their children. As each one appeared, she was told about Annabelle's birthday party. Some were surprised, some were puzzled, but only the mother of Ethan's friend Tony said he couldn't come. Tony had a dentist appointment he couldn't get out of.

Twenty-one kids were now coming to Annabelle's party. Annabelle swallowed hard. It seemed like a very large number. She hoped Grandma wouldn't be mad at her. She really hoped Grandma wouldn't be mad at her in front of her whole class!

"Everyone can come with me," she said.

"Well, that's fine," said Mrs. Blake. "I hope you all have a very good time. I'll see you tomorrow."

The three blocks to Grandma's were a very short walk. Annabelle walked with Melissa and Melissa's mother. Melissa's mother looked exactly like Melissa, except bigger and a little fatter. When Melissa had introduced her, she had smiled and shown the exact same dimples as her daughter.

The other mothers walked along with their children, too. This made for quite a large group. People passing by turned and looked at them. Shopkeepers peered out their doors.

Annabelle felt proud. She was leading all these people to *her* party at *her* grandma's! But what if Grandma didn't want to have the party after all? What if she sent everyone away when they arrived? Grandma wouldn't do that. Not her grandma. Would she?

"Hey, Annabelle," said Ethan, "is there going to be ice cream and cake at this party? You know, a party isn't a real birthday party without ice cream and cake."

Annabelle scowled back at Ethan. "Smartypants. What else would there be?"

Annabelle made her voice sound very confident, but inside she was panicking. Would there be ice cream and cake? What would her grandmother serve? Sometimes, when she went over to visit, they had coffee cake. She wouldn't serve the whole class coffee cake, would she?

"How did you decide to have this party?" Melissa asked.

"It was Grandma's idea," said Annabelle. "Grandma loves giving parties."

Grandma lived in a big old apartment building with a doorman. The doorman in the afternoon was called Frank. Annabelle knew

him pretty well. They were even sort of friends. But when she and her group arrived outside and the mothers began deciding which of them would go up, Frank came out and said, "I'm sorry, Annabelle, you can't all stand here. You're blocking the door."

"Okay, Frank," said Annabelle nervously.

"Well, that should tell us something," said Melissa's mother. "We can't all go."

Quickly it was agreed that only Melissa's and Beth's mothers would stay. The other mothers would come back at five o'clock and wait downstairs.

A moment later, two mothers and twenty-one children were in the lobby of Grandma's apartment building. There was an old mirror, a faded Oriental rug, and some puffy-looking furniture. The two mothers and twenty-two children took up most of the rest of the space.

"Annabelle," said Frank "is your grandma expecting all these people?"

"Of course," said Annabelle.

"Well, I'd better call her on the house phone and announce you're here."

With a lump in her throat, Annabelle watched as Frank dialed her grandmother's apartment number. Grandma couldn't fail her now!

Frank announced them and listened at the receiver. Then he said, "It's fine. You can all go up."

Annabelle was so relieved, she thought she might melt into the ground. "It's the eleventh floor," she said to everyone.

They had to use both elevators twice. Even then, it was pretty

crowded. Annabelle went up in the first elevator, so she could be there to direct everyone to her grandma's apartment. Ethan, Melissa, and Melissa's mother went with her.

"Oooh," said Ethan as they passed the fifth floor, "I'm getting squooshed!"

"Me, too!" said another boy called Chris.

"You are not," said Melissa's mother, and everyone was quiet.

They gathered in the hall. There were so many of them, they almost stretched back to the elevators. Everything in the hall was pretty dingy, but Annabelle had been here before and knew how different it was inside the apartment. She rang the bell.

The door opened. Light streamed into the hall, and there was Grandma. She was large and a little heavy. She had short gray hair and glasses. She wore a pink print dress and high heels and a smile a mile wide.

"Welcome, everyone," she said, "and *Happy Birthday, Annabelle!*"

4 "This *Is* a Real Birthday Party!"

"Oh, Grandma!" said Annabelle, and hugged her.

Inside, all the furniture in the living room had been pushed back against the walls. The antique sofa with the rosewood trim, the two big wing chairs, the mahogany coffee table with the bowl of walnuts—everything had been moved to make room for a whole class of children plus two mothers.

Even with everything rearranged, Grandma's living room was beautiful. Light poured in from windows facing south and west. There was a view of the river, paintings of flowers, and a whole wall of bookshelves.

"Wow!" Melissa said as she walked in. "I like this."

"Thank you," said Grandma. "I hope you will enjoy the party."

Then she turned to the rest of the group. "Children," she said, "I know it's just after school, and you must be hungry for a snack. If you'll walk straight through into the dining room, I think you will find things you like."

Obediently, as if led by an invisible force as well as the two mothers, the children made their way to the dining room. The tall chairs had been moved back. On the table was a large white cloth. On the cloth were twenty bowls, each of them filled with a small scoop of chocolate, a small scoop of vanilla, and a small scoop of strawberry ice cream. In the middle was a big plate of cookies, a pile of napkins, and a row of spoons.

"Please help yourselves," said Grandma, serving three extra portions to account for the one extra child and two extra mothers.

Instantly, the bowls of ice cream were gone. Instantly, the cookies had gone with them. The children sat on the tall dining room chairs. They sat on the living room furniture and all over the living room floor. They got through the ice cream and cookies before you could blink an eye.

"This is really good ice cream," said a girl named Stephanie.

"I don't like strawberry," said Chris.

"Then don't eat the strawberry," said Melissa's mother.

"I wonder if there's going to be cake," said Ethan. "A party's not a real birthday party without a cake."

Annabelle and Melissa were sitting in the two big wing chairs over in the corner. It was funny, because usually, when Annabelle came to visit, she and her grandma sat in those chairs. Annabelle was also wondering if there was going to be a birthday cake. She didn't especially care what Ethan thought, but it was true that a birthday party wouldn't seem right without a birthday cake.

"I love your grandma's apartment," said Melissa. "Wouldn't it be fun if we could come visit every day after school?"

Annabelle smiled. "I'd like that."

Just then a commotion began in the dining room. The kids were whispering. Someone gasped.

Out of the kitchen came Grandma, carrying a huge cake. Written across the vanilla frosting in chocolate letters were the words, HAPPY BIRTHDAY, ANNABELLE. In a circle in the middle were seven glowing birthday candles with one to grow on.

Grandma stood in the doorway between the dining room and the living room and sang "Happy Birthday."

When everyone had finished singing "Happy Birthday" to Annabelle, Grandma put the cake on the table. Annabelle ran up, made a wish, and noisily blew out the candles. Then she turned and bowed.

The children clapped. Grandma helped Annabelle cut the first piece of cake. Then she served the rest on paper plates and handed out forks and cups of milk. The cake disappeared about as fast as the ice cream and cookies.

Ethan settled back down into his place on the floor in the living room. He took a big bite of cake. "Mmmmm," he said, rolling his eyes, "this *is* a real birthday party!"

"The filling's strawberry," said Chris. "I don't like strawberry."

"Then don't eat the filling," said Melissa's mother.

Annabelle laughed. She was very glad that everything was working out so well, but she wondered how Grandma had been able to buy all that ice cream and bake a cake for her in such a short time. When Melissa had to go to the bathroom, Annabelle sneaked into the kitchen.

On the counter was a box from the Royale Bakery. Written on the box was "Happy Birthday, Prudence," but Prudence had been crossed out and Annabelle written in.

Annabelle remembered that her name on the cake had looked a little smudged. She was sad that the cake hadn't been baked for her, but she was also pleased that her grandma was so clever.

She ran back out into the living room as Grandma was saying "I'm sorry, children, but I don't have any games in the house. You'll have to think of something else to do yourselves."

"Hide and seek!" said Annabelle. "That's a fun game!"

"I didn't think you children still played that," said Grandma.

"We do!" everyone shouted.

"Annabelle's got to be it," said Melissa. "It's *her* birthday!"

"Well, fine," said Grandma. "I don't know where all of you are going to hide, but I'll let you use both bedrooms as long as you're careful."

Annabelle chose her wing chair as home base. When she'd counted to a hundred, everyone was hidden. Going room to room, she found everyone except Ethan. Suddenly he popped up from behind the sofa and raced for home base! He was going so fast, he didn't notice the bowl of walnuts on the coffee table. His arm knocked against it. Suddenly there were walnuts all over the floor.

"Nuts!" he shouted, and began stamping on them.

Chris joined in. Other children began stamping, too.

The two mothers were in the kitchen with Grandma. Now all three adults came racing out.

"Stop!" Grandma said sternly.

The children stopped.

"I'm glad you've all enjoyed yourselves," said Grandma, "but now it's time to go home. First, though, the children who stamped on the nuts will apologize, and then they will help clean up the mess."

Ethan, Chris, and the other boys and girls lined up in front of Grandma. "I'm sorry, Mrs. Fields," each one said in turn. Then they crouched down and picked up all the nuts and nutshells. Grandma gave them a box to put everything in.

By then it was five o'clock and time to leave anyway. Annabelle, of course, was staying a little later, so everyone thanked her and her grandma for a wonderful party. Melissa whispered, "I can't wait to see you tomorrow."

As Ethan said good-bye, he shook Annabelle's hand and grinned sheepishly. "I had a very good time," he said. "I'm sorry I messed up."

"It's okay now," said Annabelle. She smiled back.

And then everyone was gone, and Grandma was saying, "Sweetheart, come talk."

They moved the living room furniture back into place. They sat in the two wing chairs. Annabelle knew what was coming.

Grandma said, "Annabelle, I was very glad to have your party, but it was wrong not to ask me first and wrong to say it was your birthday when it wasn't."

Annabelle started to cry. "Everything was so nice at school, I just, I just wanted—"

Grandma took her in her lap and hugged her. "I know, but tomorrow you will have to explain."

"I can't."

"Yes, you can," said Grandma, "and I'm going to help you."

5 Nothing To Hide

"I'm going to bake a batch of cookies," Grandma went on, "I may even use some of these specially cracked walnuts in the batter. I'm going to give the cookies to you to take to school. Before you explain, you can offer them to the class. There's just one condition. Nobody eats any cookies until after lunch."

"Thanks, Grandma," said Annabelle, "but I *can't* say anything to my class. Maybe I won't go back to school. I'll get sick or something."

"You have to tell the truth," said Grandma.

Annabelle sat for a moment, wrestling with her embarrassment. She knew her grandmother was right. "Okay," she said finally, "I'll do it."

"Good," said Grandma. "Let's bake cookies."

They went into the kitchen. Grandma got out the cookie sheets and mixed the batter. She added chocolate chips and some of the walnuts after rinsing them carefully.

"Are chocolate chip cookies okay?" she asked Annabelle.

"Yes, yum," said Annabelle.

She helped Grandma plop the cookies on the sheets and put them in the oven. While they were baking, Grandma said how delighted she was that Annabelle and her parents were now living nearby and that the children in her new class seemed really nice. "Except, perhaps, that boy Ethan," she added.

Annabelle blushed. "Ethan's not so bad."

"Do I detect more than a passing interest in that area?"

"I don't know. He's just neat."

Then the cookies were ready. They smelled delicious, and when they had cooled for a few minutes, Grandma popped the first one into Annabelle's mouth.

"They're great!" said Annabelle, devouring it.

"Thank you, child. Now off you go."

Grandma packed the cookies in a bag, led Annabelle to the door, and gave her a big kiss. "You're terrific," she said. "Now be sure and let me know how everything goes."

"I will," said Annabelle. "Thanks, Grandma."

All the way home, she thought about how much she loved her grandma. All the way home, she worried about what she could say at school tomorrow. "The truth," Grandma had said. She guessed that would have to be it.

It seemed awfully hard, though. She got home, went straight to her room, and sat in her big chair with her arm around her favorite teddy bear, Buster. Maybe it *would* be better if she didn't go to school again.

Over dinner, her parents wanted to know all about her first day. She told them how great everything was and how much she liked Mrs. Blake. Then she said a few of her classmates had come back to Grandma's with her.

"Grandma must have loved that," said Dad.

"She did," said Annabelle. "She even baked some cookies for me to bring to school tomorrow."

"How lovely," said Mom. "We really must visit her this weekend."

"That's a good idea," said Annabelle.

She got back to her room as quickly as she could. At least she'd avoided the details. There wasn't any homework on the first day of school, but what would she do now? She was as nervous as she'd been last night.

She looked out the window for a while. She changed into more comfortable clothes. She played some games with her dolls and Buster. She tried a couple of books. Then she decided to go to bed.

Her parents were watching TV in the living room. She went in and hugged them. Then she brushed her teeth, put on her nightie, and climbed under the covers.

It was the same as last night. She couldn't sleep. Images of laughing classmates danced in her head. She tried not to cry again, but she didn't quite succeed.

In the morning she felt tired but determined. It was a little chilly, so she put on her new pink sweater and a pair of jeans.

Then she had her breakfast and said to her mother, "I think I'll walk to school by myself today, Mom."

"Sounds good to me," said Mom.

All the way there, Annabelle went over in her mind how she would just go up to Mrs. Blake, ask if she could talk to the class, stand up tall, and explain how she had liked everyone so much and had gotten carried away.

Then she was there, clutching the bag of cookies. She walked up the steps, pushed open the heavy glass door, stood in the hall, and froze. She couldn't possibly do any of those things. What she wanted to do was hide.

She hurried past Mrs. Blake's classroom door. She didn't know where she would go, but there had to be somewhere. She passed the art room, the cafeteria, and the library.

The library! She tried the door. It was open. She peered inside. Mr. Ryan, the librarian, was standing behind the counter. He was wearing his bifocals and seemed totally absorbed in a page of notes he held in his hand.

Annabelle tiptoed past him. She tiptoed all the way across the room to the stacks. Then she crouched down in the fiction section, between letters K and N.

It was almost eight-thirty. How long could she hide here before the first library group came in? What would happen when they found her? There were lots of interesting titles on the shelves, but she was so afraid of making noise, she didn't dare look at any.

She heard the door to the library open. Then she heard a familiar voice.

"Hi, Mr. Ryan," said the voice, "I found this library book near the water fountain, and I thought you'd want it back."

"Thank you, Melissa," said Mr. Ryan, "that's very kind of you. How was your first day in second grade?"

"It was great, but mostly because of this new girl called Annabelle. She's cute and funny, and she did this really neat thing. Just before school let out, she said it was her birthday and invited everyone in the class to her grandma's house for a party. All the kids knew it probably wasn't her birthday. Nobody forgets to mention their birthday for the *whole day,* not even on the first day of school. It was just such a neat thing. And then we got to her grandma's, and there really was a party and we all had a wonderful time."

"Melissa!" Annabelle shouted. She raced out from the stacks and threw her arms around Melissa's neck.

Melissa hugged her back. "Annabelle, what are you doing in the library?"

"Is it true?" said Annabelle, "those things you just said to Mr. Ryan, is it all true?"

"Of course it's true. Everyone knew it couldn't be your birthday, and everyone had a great time."

"And you still want to be my friend?"

"Sure. Didn't I say so?"

Mr. Ryan readjusted his bifocals. "I think you girls better get to class. It's past eight-thirty."

"Oh, yes," said Annabelle. "Oh, thank you, Mr. Ryan," she said, though they hadn't been properly introduced.

Annabelle and Melissa walked down the hall arm in arm.

Annabelle explained everything. Melissa thought it was all very funny, that Annabelle's plan would be perfectly fine. When they reached their classroom, the other kids were already in their seats.

Annabelle walked right up to Mrs. Blake. "My grandma has baked the class these cookies," she said, handing over the bag, "but no one can eat any until after lunch."

"Why, thank you, Annabelle," said Mrs. Blake, "and thank you to your grandma from the whole class."

"Now I'd like to speak to the whole class," said Annabelle.

Mrs. Blake looked surprised. "Certainly," she said. "Quiet, please, class. Annabelle wants to say something to all of you."

Annabelle stood up straight and tall. Everyone listened as she told the truth. Halfway through she noticed Ethan give her the thumbs-up sign, and she smiled at him. When she was finished, the whole class cheered!

"That was wonderful, Annabelle," said Mrs. Blake. "We're really proud to have you here in second grade."

"Thanks," said Annabelle. "I'm glad to be here, too." Then she grinned. "But you still can't have any cookies until after lunch."